GURU GOBIND SINGH

His Life Sketch

MAVEN BOOKS

GURU GOBIND SINGH
His Life Sketch

Sher Singh

MAVEN BOOKS

Chennai   Tirunelveli   New Delhi

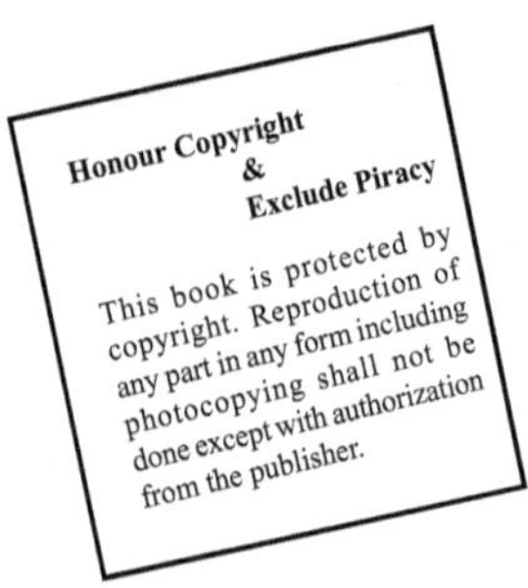

MAVEN BOOKS

An Imprint of MJP Publishers

ISBN 978-93-5527-299-7 **Maven Books**

All rights reserved   No. 44, Nallathambi Street,
Triplicane,
Chennai 600 005

MJP 1511   © Publishers, 2023

Publisher : C. Janarthanan

Publisher's Note

The legacy of a country is in its varied cultural heritage, historical literature, developments in the field of economy and science. The top nations in the world are competing in the field of science, economy and literature. This vast legacy has to be conserved and documented so that it can be bestowed to the future generation. The knowledge of this legacy is slowly getting perished in the present generation due to lack of documentation.

Keeping this in mind, the concern with retrospective acquiring of rare books has been accented recently by the burgeoning reprint industry. Maven Books is gratified to retrieve the rare collections with a view to bring back those books that were landmarks in their time.

In this effort, a series of rare books would be republished under the banner, "Maven Books". The books in the reprint series have been carefully selected for their contemporary usefulness as well as their historical importance within the intellectual. We reconstruct the book with slight enhancements made for better presentation, without affecting the contents of the original edition.

Most of the works selected for republishing covers a huge range of subjects, from history to anthropology. We believe this reprint edition will be a service to the numerous researchers and practitioners active in this fascinating field. We allow readers to experience the wonder of peering into a scholarly work of the highest order and seminal significance.

Maven Books

GURU GOBIND SINGH AS BORN LEADER OF MANKIND.

1666—1708 A. D.

Patna life of the Guru Guru Gobind Singh was born at Patna. Poh Sudi 7th 1723 Vikrami, 1666 A. D. to Mother Gujri, when his father, Guru Teg Bahedur, was absent in Assam where he had gone in connection with a peaceful mission to a prince of that province. The first few years of the babe's life were spent at Patna which is, therefore, an important "Throne" in the annals of Sikh history. The early life of Guru Gobind Singh recalled the innocent revelries of Krishna for he had won the hearts of the people, both young and old, including Raja Fateh Chand Maini, at that tender age. There was some hidden charm in his radiating face which made him at once the idol of Patna where he lived and moved like an angel wooing, bewitching and comforting every one with whom he came in contact. Sometimes, he would dart arrows from his blue bow and knock potsherds in innocent glee, but very often he would divide his mates into two groups and engage them in contests of skill and power. Hundreds of boys followed at his heel and he would march through the lanes of Patna like a victorious general parading his troops. The Guru mixed with every one, loved every one and although he was only a child, yet many a parent used to look upon him as their Redeemer, for all that he did, appeared to be a foretaste of what was coming ahead. Years afterwards, when his Patna disciples came to his sequestered corner in the Siwaliks namely the city of Bliss, they found him the same charming youth darting mirth and joy all around; his characteristic Patna whoop would often throw all in joyful confusion in which every one forgets himself and rises superior to the world and its worries.

The Spiritual magnet attracts spiritual needles.

When he was six years old, the party moved towards Anandpur stopping at Lakhnaur in the Ambala District where also he became the centre of village life. Pir Araf Din who was held in high esteem by the local people once said his prayer facing eastwards instead of looking towards Mecca, and when he was asked to explain, he stated how in his ecstatic dreams he was attracted towards this Divine Light which coming from the east in Patna was resident at Lakhnaur. The Pir soon met the Guru and bowed before him and asked his disciples to do the same.

Sayyed Bhikhan Shah another renowned Muslim Faqir also came and met the Guru being somehow attracted towards Him as a gignatic magnet attracts little needles. The Faqir sent for two little pitchers and placed them before the Guru; the Guru sent for a third and having first placed a hand on each, then covered the third with both hands. This brought tears of joy to the Faqir who explained to his followers that his test showed to him that a unique leader of mankind had been born. For by covering the pitchers, he had shown that Hindus and Mohammedans would be equally dear to him, but that he would bring into being a new dispensation where every one could live and move as a free man. These and other incidents in which religious leaders of advanced old age flocked to a boy who was hardly able to talk, show that there

(4)

was something inborn in him which made
him at once a dynamo of spiritual life, which
dynamo was destined to become a centre of
New life in India. Some such fascination
irresistibly drew the wizards of the East towards Palestine where Jesus lay in the corn-
bin, and we find the same phenomenon repea-
ted whenever and wherever a spiritual prodi-
gy is born. Here was then an extraordinary
little child. the only son of the Guru, destined
to become the tenth and the last of the Sikh
Gurus.

When he started towards Anandpur, the
whole of the city poured out in thousands to
meet him and receive him. His education
began here which included thorough study
of the sacred book, besides proficiency in
Sanskrit and Persian. Although the Guru
became well versed in all of these languages,
yet the Patna dialect which he learnt first in
his life left a life-long impress on him, and his
sacred compositions were hence couched more
in Brij-Basha than in Punjabi.

Deputation of Kashmiri Pandits and Martyrdom of Guru Tegh Bahadur The Guru was hardly nine years old when a deputation of distressed Kashmiri Pandits sought shelter at the feet of Guru Tegh Bahadur. The policy of religious persecution which Aurangzeb pursued had converted practically the whole of Kashmir, and now only a little colony of Brahmins remained who came to the Guru to help them or else they were also bound to be wiped out from existence. The tale of woe related by them brought tears to the eye of everyone who heard it; it was clear that some drastic action was required. The Guru heard it all and felt more meditative than ever before. The little child sitting at the feet of his father and Master was all eyes and all ears, he felt what was passing in the mind of his father and was engrossing his attention: "What is it, dear father, which is enshrouding thine holy face in care and gloom?" asked the little son in earnest accents. The father said: "We are up against hard times; the rulers have forgotten their duty to the ruled and are treating them not like men but as wild beasts.

(6)

Such a state of brutality cannot be endured
any longer. What cannot be mended must
be ended. But this requires a sacrifice, the
sacrifice of the purest and the whitest soul."
The child listened, and then darted out at
once " Papa, that is quite true, but who can
be holier than your august head." To Guru
Teg Bahadur, this talk did not come as a
surprise for he did not expect anything less
from his only son. but it did come to him as a
testimony of the fact that a soul was there
equal in depth and height to his own, and
that he could now do what was the pressing
need of the hour, leaving the future in the
hands of the boy who had already shown his
mettle and could be expected to discharge
the'onerous duties of his office as befit:ed
the spiritual leader of the Sikhs. Guru Teg
Bahadur repaired to Delhi where he was
offered the usual alternative either to accept
the ruler's religion or be beheaded. He
accepted the latter and this passed away the
holiest man of the times. A storm of dust
swift over Delhi that night, but little did the
Mughal Emperor know that this storm was
destined also to carry off the Mughal Empire

which was now withering and before long would be like a dead leaf carried off by a whiff of wind. The Master passed away at Delhi—but He yet lived at Anandpur!

Annadpur, the City of Bliss. The matter does not rest there. Men sighed and cried but angels on high revelled in joy. For, they knew that dark clouds are really harbingers of new light and life. It may be that the horizon would remain clouded for sometime, but as surely as the day follows the night, better conditions were bound to prevail. The new sun was now destined to rise at Anandpur, the martyred Guru's quite retreat at the foot of the Himalayas. The site chosen by the Guru was, indeed, an hermitage beyond the din and turmoil of the busy work-day world. Here, the weary and woe-begone came and sought refuge at the feet of the Master, the sick were healed and nursed, the hungry were fed, the unlettered were imparted instruction in hoary lore. When Guru Gobind Singh assumed the reins of the spiritual suzereinty, he decided to turn Anandpur into a veritable Paradise. Anandpur became a university where training was given in religion as well as in arms. The Guru's free kitchen ministered freely to the body while his discourses and his Dewans ministered to the soul of those who flocked to him from all corners of the Punjab. His Durbars were devoted to divine worship and many years were passed in narrating to the people the exploits of their forefathers including Rama and Krishna. The bards who attended the Guru's court, composed and recited poetry and thus the Lord's praise was the chief education of the Guru and those who clustered round him. He had come to establish the Kingdom of Heaven on earth, and at Anandpur, the people did feel that they were really in new surroundings, and that they had what they missed in the din and bustle of city life. The Guru was serene and calm like the placid waters of Mansarovar, and his tranquil face rained bliss on one and all. Anandpur became a place for pilgrimage and a congregating centre for the learned and woe-beladen.

Raja Rattan Rai, son of Raja Ram Rai of

Assam whom the Nineth Guru had blessed with this son, came to the Guru at Anandpur and as a token of his gratitude brought many presents including a white-striped elephant which waved a fan or *chauri* over the Guru, held a jug of water in his trunk while the Guru's feet were washed, wiped his feet with a towel, fetched his arrows and did many other things which astonished all those who saw the elephant. This elephant soon became an apple of discord for Raja Bhim Chand of Bilaspur who saw the elephant asked for its loan meaning never to return the animal. On the Guru's refusal to part with Rattan Rai's gift, Bhim Chand's wrath knew no bounds. Other hill chiefs who were already displeased with the Guru for letting *Sudras* mix with the Keshtriyas and bringing them to the same level, also joined Raja Bhim Chand. The discontented *Masands* who were either dispossessed or were not feeling safe under the Guru's vilentage also conspired against the Guru. Thus friction ensued between the Guru and the neighbouring hill Rajas, and as it had become necessary to do something in

(10)

self-defence, hence the Guru selected a beau-
tiful spot on the banks of the Jamna and
erected there a fortress called Paunta.

The battle of Bhangani The hill chiefs of Kangra,
under the leadership of Bhim
Chand, marched on the Guru and a fierce
battle ensued at the village Bhangani, close
to Paunta. The Guru's army consisted of
local cattle-grasers, confectioners, coblers etc.,
besides a few mercenaries who were Pathans.
While the latter deserted the field, the Sikh
soldiery did wonders killing many a hill chief.
Sayyed Budhu Shah who was an ardent
admirer of the Guru himself joined the conflict
and two of his sons fell on the field never to
rise again. The victory of the Guru was
complete, the hill chiefs who tested the
Master's steel at Bhangani did not dare to
molest him in open warfare any longer.
The Guru's army, drunk with victory was
enrayed, at the treachery of erstwhile friend
Raja Fateh Shah of Srinagar, and sought the
Guru's permission to attack him and bring
him captive before the Guru. But the Guru
did not fight to conquer, he fought only in

self-defence, so he restrained his army and returned without even an inch of territory. After a short stay at Paunta, the Guru's army returned to Anandpur where once more the spiritual atmosphere was restored, and the soldiers doffed their uniforms to till land, to toil. and to imbibe *Nam-dan* at the feet of the Master.

Conflict with the Mughal Ruler: the Sieage of Anandpur. The abode of Bliss became as of old a centre of good-will and peace. Messengers went out in all directions with the message of the Guru and the popularity of the town increased. The first to receive this message were, of course, the neighbouring hill chiefs, some of whom became friendly, but many of them who were blinded by deep-rooted prejudices and who could not feel the beauty of mankind coming to its own, looked at him with scorn and scoffed at him. Thus, two cross currents were set up at Anandpur. On the one hand, there was peaceful Movement which brought equality and fraternity among the masses, turning Anandpur into veritable land of bliss. On the other hand, the ani-

mosity of the Hill-Cains was aroused, as they
could not brook the idea of seeing their brothers attain their full manhood. The fight
at Bhangari had driven the current of ani-
mosity underground and when other alternatives failed, the hill chiefs went and sought
the aid of Emperor, Arungzeb to oust the
Guru from his citedel. The emperor who was
watching the little Guru ever since his father
was beheaded, was only too anxious to snatch
at the opportunity of nipping the Khalsa
commonwealth in the bud. His reporter had
already informed him how on the eventful
day of Baisakhi Samet 1756 (1699 A. D.), the
great Guru had selected his five lieutinants
Panj Piyare who had gone through the ordeal
of blood, and no less than 20,000 people stood
up in that gathering and promised to lay
down their life in the fulfilment of his divine
mission, and the number had since swelled to
80,000 and was ever on the increase. Aurangzeb was at that time in the Deccan. He ordered his Viceroys of Sarhind and Lahore to
march at once against the Guru which they
did besieging Annandpur in 1701 A. D. The

Sikhs fought with dauntless courage, verified by the unfluttering flame of *Nam*, but the odds were quite disproportionate, for a small colony of resident Sikhs was surrounded by bees of Mughal disciplined forces including hill chiefs of Kangra, Nurpur, Chamba etc. Nothing daunted, the battle continued. Hunger, death and disease worked havoc in the colony, yet this dismayed not the Guru when force failed. The unscrupulous foe then took a treacherous vow and promised on Kuran and cow to give the Guru safe conduct, provided he evacuated the Anandpur fort. This vow had its desired effect.

The first of Mugh: the forty deserters.
Mata Gujri, mother of Guru Gobind Singh. who felt for the sufferings of the famished garrison told her son: "my son, leave the fort and save your people. The Mughals have promised not to molest us. and it is no good courting sure death." The Guru, however, knew better for oaths on holy books can as well be made and un-made by unscrupulous enemies. Taking the eve from the mother, some of the wavering Sikhs also came forward and said:

"We are dying of hunger, O True King, let us go." The Guru told them it was not safe to leave Anandpur and to be at the mercy of the Mughal forces. He asked them to wait for a week more in which time he hoped, the machinations of the enemy would themselves become clear. But even this little period was too much for them and forty out of the thinned ranks decided to desert the Guru, so they went and informed him accordingly. The Guru told them to do what they liked if they would not abide by the command of the Master, but in that case he demanded from them a written declaration that they were no longer his Sikhs. The forty were determined to do anything to save their life, so after a little pause and searching of heart, they went and handed over the desired paper to him saying: "Take it. You are not our Guru and we are not your Sikhs." As he extended his arm to receive the paper, his lofty plume waved in the air and rubbed against the rich trapping overhead, for the Guru jumped to receive the paper. 'Go ye then, and do what ye like" said he, folding and pulling the paper in his

vest pocket. They had been away from their
hearts and homes for long and now they expected a hearty welcome from their families.
But their families had already known of their
infidelity, as the news of their desertion ran
like into fire. Headed by mother Bhago, their
sisters, mothers and daughters came and met
the party at a distance from the village. Lady
Bhago who was dressed in male costume
addressed them and said "O cowards, ye have
turned traitors at the time of dire necessity.
Ye are not men but women, come sit at home
cook and spin, we will go and fight in your
stead." The telling words of mother Bhago
brought them to their self again, and shame
faced they returned to the battle-field once
more. They wanted to seek forgiveness for
their desertion, but how could they face him
with guilty conscience. So they decided to
die for him and to wring forgiveness by their
sacrifice. The Forty now set out in search for
him as charged men.

Muktsar and
the forty immor-
tal.
The Guru had left Anandpur
by that time and had reached
Khidrana, after many wanderings and when he

was there, he was informed that the enemy was coming towards him. The Guru mounted up his blue steed, took up his bow and arrows and went up a sand hill from where he watched the enemy. But, the enemy instead of marching on the Guru had first to fight the forty Sikhs who had just returned and were now encamped near a little pond. Wazir Khan, the Commander of the Royal force, saw the encampment from a distance and attacked the same, but, in return, they were greeted with ceaseless vollies of arrows and bullets shot by the forty. Although the odds were over-whelming. the forty decided to fight viliantly. The ground was littered with mutilated heads, arms and limbs. The intrepedity of these struck terror in the heart of mercenary soldiers of the Mughal army. Wazir Khan called a council of war. Kapura, a Government agent informed them that no water was available in vicinity and it was not advisable to risk life here, for the exact number of the Khalsa was not known. So Wazir Khan ordered retreat. The Guru had watched the whole scene with his own eyes, he had seen the Khalsa fight and die with their faces towards the enemy. He knew who they were so he rushed towards them on his blue steed. He found all the Forty there, on the ground, breathless or on the point of death. He began to search them one by one, from amongst the dead. He took each individual head in his lap, wiped it and kissed it. He ·came across one who was yet breathing, albeit heavily, recognising him, the Master said: "Mohan Singh, my son, is it you, look unto me." The martyr at once recognised his Master, but his eyes were downcast, because the scene at Anandpur still rankled in his eyes When he saw the kindly Master, a stream of tears trickled in his eyes, his cheeks flushed and he tried in vain to move his mutilated body to touch the Master's feet. The Master said: "Mohan Singh, you have conquered me. I am pleased with your devotion. It is never too late to mend." Mohan Singh mumbled: "Master, we are sinners, we deserted you at the time of dire necessity forgive us, save us, tear that scraf of paper we handed over to you on that eventful, and embrace the forty more."

The Master did what he was asked to do, and
he took out that ray which he treasured in his
vest pocket, and tore it: the *Be-dawa*. The
forty were thus saved, they became Immortal
Mukte, and the gory ground which they beanti-
fied with their blood is now known as *Muktsar*.
The Tank was rebuilt and is known as the
Tank of Salvation. The Master said: "Those
who bathe in it on the 1st of Magh, shall be
re-born ever as Muktas of old." The episode
of Muktsar is a silver lining to the dark cloud
which enveloped the Sikhs at Anandpur and
which dogged them in all their wanderings in
the sandy plains and dunes of the Malwa.
Mother Bhago is the *Arundhati* of Sikh history,
faithful, loyal and brave such as no earth-born
ever was.

Siege of Anandpur (Continued.) Anandpur siege had another
silver lining to its dark cloud for
the Mughal Commander-in-chief namely Saiy-
yed Khan who came as an enemy became a
friend and disciple of the Guru after personally
experiencing the Guru's powers in the field.
How this unexpected miracle came to pass in
a battle-field is worthy of special mention and

we will refer to it in detail later on describing the Master's magnetic personality. Here, it is enough to state that Anandpur, the city of bliss, did have its charming and magnetic atmosphere which could not but attract and influence even the avowed enemies of the Guru. When the Guru left Anandpur in 1704 A. D. he threw practically all valuables in the river, and it was only the literary treasure and little cash that was taken. The Guru left the City of Peace in bliss for hymns were chanted and the word resounded in the air when the fortress was evacuated. When the besiegers learnt that the Guru had left, they lost no time in chasing them. although they had solemnly promised not to do so. Severe fighting ensued on the banks of the *Sarsa nadi* and in the confusion that followed, the Guru's mother and his two youngest sons escaped with only one attendant namely Gangu. The Guru with his two eldest sons and a little party of Sikhs made towards Ropar. Most of the Manuscripts which were a result of twenty years' prolonged labour were either lost in the affray or washed away by the river and the *Dasam-Granth* which contains the

Guru's word, is but a dwindled part of the gigantic labour of the Guru on the banks of the Jumna and Sutlej.

Siege of Chamkaur.   Hemmed in from front and behind the Guru hurried towards Chamkaur where he occupied the mud-built house of a jat located on an eminence. The enemy surrounded the house and tried to force open the gate. The arrows and bullets of the Guru and his Sikhs, however, did not let them come so near. The missilies of the enemy fell thick like hailstorm on the thinned band of the Khalsa. The Guru was seated on the sandhill and was darting his gold-headed arrows right and left which worked havoc among the wavering and chicken-hearted hill chiefs. The Khalsas were dying one by one but they knew that there was no ordinary cause. They were fighting practically single-handed against heavy odds because they were fighting the *asures*, and the cup of martyrdom was ready for them. The Guru watched the battle with divine calmness. So his master mind, the whole thing was a melodreme, in which he, his sons and disciples, one and all, had to play their part and that effectively. So when he found his ranks thinned, he called for his own sons. His eldest son known as *Ajit* or unconquerable, said "Dear father, I cannot be conquered, let me go out first, to join my brothers that have gone before." The Guru knew that to send out his son would be court to sure death, but he asked his younger son Prince Jujhar to follow his brother. The younger one was hardly 14; the Guru dressed his turban with his own hand and gave him a little sword, a mere cutless. Both the princes advanced to measure their steel with heavy odds in front. Ajit performed prodigies of velour; his younger brother had never seen such an odd before. His heart sank under the deafering roar of cannon, and felt a lump rising in his throat and his lips were parched with thirst. He came back to the Guru to beg for a cup of water. But the Guru said: Dear Jujhar go where thy brother Ajit has gone, he has the cup of nectar ready for you which will quench your thirst." The prince did not wait for another hint and flashing his cutless, rushed into the enemy's rank, killing and being killed, blood strickling through his elastic veins and turning the ground purple. The Guru's face was jubilant, and his countenance breathed unearthly satisfaction. Thus ended another memorable day as much famous in Sikh history as the Maghi-day of Muktsar fame.

When the brave boys had shed their blue blood, the remaining Khalsa gathered together and passed a resolution (*Gurmatta*) that the Guru must be saved at all cost, so obeying the *Panth*, the Guruship was entrusted to the Holy word, and Guru Gobind Singh escaped from Chamkaur accompanied by Daya Singh, Dharm Singh and a few others. The Sikhs who remained in the fort put the Guru's plume on the head of Sant Singh so that the Mughal forces thought that the Guru is still at Chamkaur, his head was cut off and taken to Delhi to regale the eyes of the Emperor. But the Guru was yet up and doing, and he was free from the grip of the Mughal hands.

Murder of the innocent children: Bhujangi Khalsa.

The remaining two sons of the Guru namely Zorawar Singh and Fateh Singh who barely 9 and 7 respectively fell in the death-trap of Gangu who in order to get hold of the cash with Mother Gujri, handed them over to the Governor of Sirhand, namely Wazir Khan. The usual alternatives of death or acceptance of Islam were offered to them. They remained undaunted and calm and refused to change their religion, on the other hand the loud shout of *Sat Sri Akal* rent the court-room with deafering cry. The Wazir of the Viceroy Suchanand, a Brahmin, told him that these are the progeny of cobra and should be smothered; Nawab of Malerkotla interceded for the innocent children. Ultimately they were bricked alive when their blood, flesh and bones were utilized in place of concrete and mortar. This was on 13th Poh Sambat 1762 (1705 A. D.), another red-letter day in the history of the Sikhs. The dauntless mien of the Guru's sons has since given another meaning to the word *Bhujhangi*: ' cobra's progeny,' for it is now used in reverent terms for all young-Sikhs, who are expected to come up to the standard of Fateh Singh and Zorawar Singh. Forster, an English historian has well said, that Wazir Khan, the Governor of Sarhind "sullied the reputation he had acquired in this service (that of persecuting the Guru) by putting to death, in cold blood, the two younger sons of Govind Singh." The Guru's mother when she heard this terrible news died of a broken heart. Thus all the four children, his father and mother were sacrificed by the Guru at the altar of Indian liberty.

The Guru heard this astounding news when he was in company of Rai Kalha, near Machhiwara, and although the letter wept tears of blood, yet the Guru sat unmoved, unruffled for he was above all mundane shocks. But at that time the cosmic impulse arose in him and involuntarily he took hold of his poniard and with its tip dug the root of a shrub that grew nearby. When Rai Kalha asked him the meaning of this spontaneous gesture, he said firmly: "My sons still live, they live in the would-be Khalsa

Commonwealth which will rise on the ashes of the Mughal Empire which is uprooted to-day, even as that little shrub is uprooted by my poniard." This was a great prophetic foreboding, and the fall of Mughal Empire may be said to synchromise from the day when the cold-blooded murder of innocent children took place. It is the blackest spot in the Mughal history, darker than Black Hole or Jallianwala episodes in Indian history left.

The epistle of victory': Zafar-nama. One should have expected that the Guru should have felt most distressed at about this time of his life, for by now he had lost his four sons, the forty were gone, hundred and thousands of his followers were gone, his father and mother were no more, his wife was weaned from him, and from her children for all time, but it was at this time 1706 A. D. that he wrote from a village known as Dina his celebrated epistle: *Zafarnama* which literally means : the *Epistle of victory*, not of defeat. This is very characteristic of the Saint-General every line is pregnant with life and righteous indignation and the Guru tells

Aurangzeb that far from his being a follower of the Prophet, Aurangzeb was one of the foremost melingners of Mohammed, for he did not understand the A. B. C. of Religion. The Guru was not an idol-worshipper, he aimed at removing untouchability and bringing India back to its pristone glory. In this work, he was thwarted by the hill chiefs who conspired and intrigued to bring in the Mughal Emperor. The latter did not understand the move of the Hill Rajas, and gave in. This was not all. He has written several autograph letters to the Guru in which he took an oath on Qoran that the Guru and his Khal-a would not be molested if they evacuated Anandpur, and yet at Chamkaur and all along the route, the Mughal hordes had done their worst to destroy the Khalsa, they had even beheaded Sant Singh who looked like the Guru. Refering to the murder of his sons, the Guru remarked: "What though my four sons were killed, I remain behind like a coiled snake? What bravery is it to quench a few sparks of life? Thou art merely exciting a raging fire all the more.... As thou didn't forget thy word on that day, so will

God thee." Such is the righteous strain of this epistle that even the stone-hearted Aurangzeb could not but be moved. As to what effect it had on Aurangzeb will be discussed in detail separately, here it is enough to state that these outward reverses had made the Guru all the more resilient, all the more steeled to his iron resolve *i. e.* to win the cause of righteousness. He wrote in Vichitra Natak, that the greater the apparent reverse; the greater the righteous recoil (ਜਬਈ ਬਾਣ ਲਾਗੈ ਤਬਈ ਰੋਸ ਜਾਗੈ), and the celebrated epistle that he wrote in rhymed Persian is a true index of the greatness of the Guru. Mark Napoleon in a sequestered cell at St. Helena, he feels despondent, care-worn, bent on committing suicide, on the other hand, the Guru writes the Epistle of Victory on the day when his outward fortune is at lowest ebb—he is most himself when he is bent surrounded by the world !

Damdama or breathing place, and dictation of the *Ad-Granth.* The Guru moved on from Dina to Kot Kapura, Dhilwan and while en-route witnessed the battle of Muktsar which was fought by the Forty on their return from home, then stopped for sometime in the *Lakhi Jungle*, so called as the Nam-nectar had transformed the sun-burnt sandy-hills of Malwa into a veritable garden of Aden. Here, many of his followers: the saint-soldiers reclustered round him. Ibrahim, a Mohammedan saint who had passed many years in austerities in this scorching plain, came to the Guru, sat at his feet, and became a full-fledged Khalsa, re-named Ajmer Singh. How did this miracle come to pass deseves detailed mention and we will refer to it later. Suffice it to say, that whenever the Guru had little breathing time, the Nam-congregations were held, religious discourses were delivered, *Asa-di-War* was sung in the morning as a matter of routine, and the Anandpur blissful atmosphere was reproduced here, there and everywhere in Majha, Malwa and as we shall see at Nander. That was the Nectar which sustained the Sikhs, which stirred them with life anew, and which made no difference to them whether they lived or died, provided they were true to

the cause that was so dear to them and of
which the Guru was the very head and heart.
In the Lakhi Jungle, the poets and songsters
sat on the sand-hills and under the scorching
rays of the sun, sang of the cool atmosphere
which *Nam* brings ; they sang *papia*—like of
the Kingdom of Heaven that is our birth-
right, if only we could apply ourselves to it.
How pleased. moved and stirred were the
disciples on seeing their Master would be
evident from the following soul-stirring
effusion of the Master which flowed out of his
lips like water coming out of gargoyle :

"When they heard the call of the Beloved
Master, even the buffaloes let drop the half-
chewn grass from their mouths, and lifted in
hurry their half-slaked lips from the pool ;

None lingered to wait for the other;
each came running all alone, such was the
over-powering force of the fascination which
overcame their heart ;

The period of fascination was over; the
Friend, the Master re-met and caressed them;
then they were relieved, comforted and great

was their rejoicing when they thanked their Lord."

This *khayal* of the Guru should be read in conjunction with another in which the pangs of the Disciples on their separation from their Beloved as described by the Guru himself thus:

"Convey unto our Beloved, the woeful tale of his disciple :
Without Thee the luxury of soft beds and of the sweet rest is galling and excruciating like a disease ;
Life in a palace is like living among adders— if Thou art away ;
The goblet of wine is like unto a cross,
The wine cup is like a sharp poniard—if Thou art away ;
Yea, without Thee, these articles of comfort choke us, kill us even as a butcher's knife ;
A pallet made of turf and straw is dearer than a silk bed, if Thou art here,
Or else the palace burneth like hell! fire—O, if Thou art away."

These two spontaneous out-pourings of love-stricken heart show that the tie which united the Guru and his disciples was not that of money, nor that of any other worldly inducement, it was that of love, sacrifice, and a love all, the yearning of re-union with the Infinite. The way to heaven was always strewn with thorns. The way to new life lay through the cross. The saint-soliders of the Guru were after this new life, bumper life which lives through life and death, through grave; yea, they were after life-eternal, hence it did not matter to them as to who fell, how many fell, for one and all did live— they lived the life-eternal which defies death, and which is the very essence of Nam-life.

From Lakhi Jungle, the other resting place was a place known as Talwandi Sabo where the Master's tent was pitched on a little mound. The Master rested here much longer, and the Anandpur atmosphere was reproduced in right earnest. Here the Guru's wife remet him and asked him "where are my Four." Pointing to hubdreds and thousands of Saint-soldiers who were congregated in that big *maidan*, the Guru said: "For these, my sons, I have sacrified the Four, what if they are gone, hundred and thousands do live. The Four are not dead; they live and play in the lap of the Father in Heaven." Such was the fascinating atmosphere of Talwandi, that the Guru called it *Kashi* of the Sikhs, the Beneres, for here poets, philosophers and mystics had flocked in hundreds to the feet of the Master. The Guru also dictated here the Ad. Granth from his memory, as Kartarpur Custodians of the Sacred Book refused to part with their copy. The new *Bir*, comprised the *Bani* of Guru Teg Bahadur, as also one *slok* of the Tenth Guru. But that *slok* is worthy of special mention in as much as, it shows how the spirit of the Epistle of victory pervades the whole of his Bani. Guru Teg Bahadur had written :

i.   "The friends and well-wishers desert us in the end, no one sticks to the last;

O Nanak, the supreme one alone is the last pillar of support in such calamity" (55)

ii.   Strength vanishes, fetters fall in our feet, there is no remedy;

O Nanak, in this dire calamity, the Supreme One comes to our aid even as He befriended the elephant when caught by the tortoise." (53)

Guru Gobind Singh interposed his own *shlok* in between which is as follows :—

"I have all the needful power, fetters fall off my feet, there is a remedy to every melody ;

O Nanak, all is in the hands of the Supreme One, who is my Friend and Suppor- ter." (54)

This *Shlok* is a eve to the whole *Bani* of the Tenth Guru, in which he expresses supreme faith in himself, in his mission and in his final victory The place where the Guru Granth was re-written is known as *Dam-dama* or the resting place.

Dalla and Sikh bravery: An example typical of Sikh attitude. While at Damdama, another scene occurred which deserves special attention as it brings out the devoted attitude of the Sikhs and their bravery in such a way as cannot be illustrated better otherwise. Dalla was a chief of Damdama and he was Moslem by faith, but

he was friendly to the Guru. Dalla had heard
of the Lord's privations, how he had lost his
sons and narrowly escaped himself through
the fidality of a few faithful friends. Dalla
touched the feet of the Master and said : "I
am really sorry my Lord, you did not inform
me, your servant. I keep always a company
of no war veterans, who wield sword with rare
dexterity and whose presence spreads panic
in the ranks of the enemy." Thus Dalla was
proceeding with his speech and pro-offer when
a visitor entered and resting his head on
Master's feet presented him a gun which he
had made himself having spent love-labour at
it for many days and nights. The Guru
accepted the offer and addressing Dalla said,
"Dalla, here is a chance, bring me one of your
men, I want to try it." Dalla was confounded
and mumbled : 'Lord, should human beings
be used as targets, who would like to die for
nothing " Dalla repaired to his camp and
in order to prove his bravado which he had
just uttered, tried to persuade one of his
followers to come. Dalla's proposition was
met with a storm of opposition in his own

ranks, and he returned to the Lord's presence with a drooping head. The Guru understood the meaning of that gesture and said to one of his attendants "Go in my camp and tell them I want one to try my new gun." The orders were conveyed. It erected a storm of confusion, all was hurly burly and about a dozen disciples reached the Guru's presence, some bare-footed, others yet binding their turban. The Guru selected one who came foremost: "Come out, you appear to be very fond of dying, stand here." The disciple stood, firm like a pillar, with his breast up-heaved, ready to receive the bullet. The Guru raised the gun and was about to move the trigger when another who had just bound his turban, rushed forward with folded hands and said: "Sir, I request a little favour." He said: "The target for your aim is my real brother. Had he been singled out for a jagir by his father or any other grant, half of the property would naturally descend to me, but now that you are confering on him the cup of immortality, I claim half of it." It amused the Lord and he said: "I grant it, come stand behind your brother, so that my bullet may deal with you both squarely, but take care that the bullet does not miss you." Both stood straight, one behind the other, over anxious to receive the shot. The Lord shouldered the gun, aimed it at them and 'click' went off the gun, but the Lord took pretty good care to pass the bullet over their heads. The Sikhs did not swerve an hair-breadth. Dalla saw the whole scene with his eyes, he was amazed, moved and changed. He longed to be one of the sikhs, a moth who would burn on the Guru's flame. He was baptized and known as Dalla Singh. The Guru told him : "your men will now have enough of exercise, but you must do what the wrestling-brothers had taught." The words had electric effect for when Banda Bahadur came to Punjab, these new-born Sikhs did prove their mettle and their worth. Thus love-conquests were made, and new desciples picked up here, there and everywhere. Hund-reds and thousands flocked to his standard, wherever he was. According to Trumpt, at Damdama alone, 1,20,000 disciples joined the

Guru.

Deccan life of the Guru. Soon after the receipt of *Zafarnama*, Aurangzeb passed away. He died in February, 1707. Bahadur Shah was then away in Afghanistan, and his younger brother, Mohammed Azim, who was with his father in Deccan, usurped the throne and took possession of the treasury. Thus Bahadur Shah who was rightful heir, was placed in the same position in which Dara Shikoh was placed by Aurangzeb. But Bahadur Shah had a strong link with Guru Gobind Singh in that his once Correspondence Secretary, namely Nand Lal, was now in the Guru's Durbar, where he wielded an influential opinion. So when the war of succession arose, Bahadur Shah approached the Guru through Nand Lal. He promised to undo all what his father had done, he promised to punish the Governor of Sirhand, he wanted to make full atonement for the wrongs of his father. Bahadur Shah knew full well that Guru Gobind Singh alone held the key to the situation for he was no ordinary man but '*Hind ka Pir*' all-India leader, above all spiritual leader, *par excellence.* The Guru whose religion recognised no difference between a Hindu and Mohammedan. and who was always ready to help the aggrieved, met Bahadur Shah at Agra where the Emperor gave him a robe of honour and solemnly promised to carry out all the promises which he made and communicated through Bhai Nand Lal. The Guru and the Emperor remained together for some-time, and then they travelled together to the south through Rajputana, reaching Nander in Hyderabad Deccan where Bahadur Shah was able to get what he wanted *i. e.* the Mughal throne. The Guru had promised to get back the throne which he did for his friend and ally. But he would not be a farther party to the subjugation of Hindu India, hence the two parted company at Nander where the Guru began to preach the Word once more, and hundreds of men flocked to his standard to hear what the Master said, to be thrilled and to be electrified Thus, Anandpur was reproduced once more on the banks of the Godavri, and even as that hallowed site was known as 'Citadel of

Peace' so this new town full of new life was re-named as Abchal-Nagar, the city Eternal. D y after day, the Guru held Nam-gathering baptized people, initiated them into his creed. The Mughal Emperor knew all this. He had promised to punish the Governors of Sirhand. to undo what his father did to the Khalsa Community at large: he could not carry out his promises, weak as he was, although he was named as 'the brave.' When a professedly brave man is coward at heart, then he becomes treacherous also, so in order to smother the still-born Voice which waxed eloquent again and again in his heart, he arranged to get the Guru murdered by a 'hired Pathan.' This diabolical deed occurred on the fifth of bright half of Katik, Sambat 1765 (A.D 1708) a year after his sojourn in that Eternal city of the South. The Guru had done good turn to the Mughal, but he was as much a traitor as Aurangzeb, although to keep appearances, he sent a doctor to dress the wound of the Guru. The wound heeled, but was re-opened when the Guru stretched his bow. Before He passed away, He held a Durbar, in which His last words were as follows:—

"The *Panth*: the Khalsa is the corporate
Guru, under the enternal guidance of the im-
personal Guru: *Granth Sahib.* If ye follow
that Divine Master, ye will never go astray!
My blessings to ye all!"

The Master passed away—He is yet with
us in the mystic Body of the *Guru-Granth*!